HEIDI HECKELBECK
and the Tie-Dyed Bunny

By Wanda Coven
Illustrated by Priscilla Burris

LITTLE SIMON

New York London Toronto Sydney New Delhi

LITTLE SIMON
An imprint of Simon & Schuster Children's Publishing Division
1230 Avenue of the Americas, New York, New York 10020
Copyright © 2014 by Simon & Schuster, Inc.
All rights reserved, including the right of reproduction in whole or in part in any form.
LITTLE SIMON is a registered trademark of Simon & Schuster, Inc., and associated colophon is a trademark of Simon & Schuster, Inc.
For information about special discounts for bulk purchases, please contact Simon & Schuster Special Sales at 1-866-506-1949 or business@simonandschuster.com.
The Simon & Schuster Speakers Bureau can bring authors to your live event. For more information or to book an event contact the Simon & Schuster Speakers Bureau at 1-866-248-3049 or visit our website at www.simonspeakers.com.
Manufactured in the United States of America 1213 FFG
First Edition 10 9 8 7 6 5 4 3 2 1
Library of Congress Cataloging-in-Publication Data
Coven, Wanda.
Heidi Heckelbeck and the tie-dyed bunny / by Wanda Coven ; illustrated by Priscilla Burris. — First edition.
pages cm. — (Heidi Heckelbeck ; 10)
Summary: Heidi is chosen to take the principal's rabbit home over Easter weekend and promises to follow all the rules, but she decides to break one and even her magic is not enough to set things right again.
ISBN 978-1-4424-8937-0 (pbk : alk. paper) — ISBN 978-1-4424-8938-7 (hc : alk. paper) — ISBN 978-1-4424-8939-4 (ebook : alk. paper) [1. Rabbits as pets—Fiction. 2. Easter—Fiction. 3. Witches—Fiction. 4. Magic—Fiction.]
I. Burris, Priscilla, illustrator. II. Title.
PZ7.C83393Hbt 2014
[Fic]—dc23
2012051745

CONTENTS

Chapter 1

THE BUNNY HOP

Boing!

Boing!

Boing!

No one could sit still in Mrs. Welli's second-grade classroom. Everyone wanted to hold Maggie. Maggie was a fluffy white bunny with bright blue eyes. She belonged to Principal Pennypacker, but sometimes he let Maggie go on classroom visits.

This week Mrs. Welli's class had Maggie. Mrs. Welli let her students take turns holding the bunny. When it was Heidi's turn, she cuddled Maggie in her arms. The other kids gathered around.

"Her fur feels like velvet," said Heidi.

Lucy Lancaster stroked Maggie's fur. "She's the softest little fluff ball in the whole world," she said.

"Let me touch her!" said Natalie Newman.

"No, I want a turn!" said Melanie Maplethorpe as she pushed her way to the front of the group.

Mrs. Welli clapped her hands.

"Everyone, take your seats," she

said. "It's time to put Maggie back in her cage. The bunny needs a rest."

Heidi slowly walked to the cage and let Maggie hop in. Then she sat down with the rest of the class.

"I have very exciting news, boys and girls," Mrs. Welli said.

The class looked eagerly at their teacher.

"Principal Pennypacker is going to pick one lucky boy or girl to take Maggie home for Easter weekend."

Everyone gasped and squealed.

"At the end of the day," Mrs. Welli continued, "the principal will draw a name from our class hat. The winner will take Maggie home tomorrow."

Mrs. Welli passed out a piece of

paper to each student in the class.

"If you'd like to take the rabbit home, please write your name on the slip of paper," she said.

Everyone began to chatter about who would get the bunny. Heidi had always dreamed of having her very own pet. *Oh, I hope I'll get the bunny,* she thought as she wrote her name on the paper. But her chances didn't seem good. *Everyone* wanted to take Maggie home.

"Come on, kids. One, two, three—all

6

eyes on me!" Mrs. Welli said.

The room quieted down.

"I know everyone's excited about the rabbit," said Mrs. Welli. "But right now I want you to line up *quietly* for art."

Everyone lined up, but it was too hard to be quiet. They chatted, giggled, and hopped like bunnies all the way down the hall.

Boing! Boing! Boing!

Chapter 2

BUNNY TALK

"Time to decorate your Easter baskets," said Mr. Doodlebee, the art teacher. "You may use stickers, markers, glitter, and gemstones."

"I love stickers," said Lucy, placing a bunny sticker on her basket.

"Gemstones are the best," said

Heidi as she glued
several purple and
emerald gems in
a checkerboard
pattern.

"That's very creative,
Heidi," said Mr. Doodlebee.

"Thanks," said Heidi,
admiring her basket.

Melanie sat next to Heidi at the table. She cleared her throat to get Mr. Doodlebee's attention. "And what do you think of MY basket?" she asked. Melanie, also known as Smell-a-nie, was usually mean to Heidi.

"Oh my!" said Mr. Doodlebee, pinching the bridge of his nose. "It's extremely sparkly."

"I know," said Melanie proudly.

"You can never have too many sparkles."

Heidi and Lucy giggled.

"What's so funny?" asked Melanie in a snooty voice.

"Your face!" said Lucy. "You have as much glitter on your face as you do on your basket."

Melanie brushed her face with the back of her hand.

"Just wait and see. The Easter Bunny is going to LOVE my basket," said Melanie. "And I'm going to get the MOST candy."

"I hope the Easter Bunny wears sunglasses," said Bruce Bickerson.

"How come?" Melanie asked.

"So he doesn't go blind when he sees your basket," said Bruce.

Heidi and Lucy giggled.

"Very funny," said Melanie. "You weirdos won't laugh when you see

how much candy I get. I'll even have
enough to share with Maggie."

"Hold on," said Lucy. "Who says
you're going to get Maggie?"

"I say so," said Melanie.

Lucy rolled her eyes.

"What makes you so sure?" asked
Stanley Stonewrecker.

"I just have a good feeling about
it," said Melanie. "That's all."

Bruce looked up from his basket.

"Did you say you are going to give CANDY to Maggie?" he asked.

"Yup," said Melanie.

"Don't you know candy is not good for rabbits?" said Bruce.

"HEL-LO!" said Melanie. "For your information, the Easter Bunny GIVES OUT candy. I'm pretty sure that means candy is okay for rabbits."

Heidi looked at Lucy.

"I'm pretty sure she's cracked," said Heidi.

The girls laughed.

AND THE WINNER IS...!

Heidi and her classmates filed back into Mrs. Welli's classroom after art. Principal Pennypacker had already arrived. He stood at the front of the room while everyone hurried to their seats.

"I hope Smell-a-nie doesn't get the

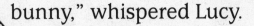

bunny," whispered Lucy.

"She'd better not," Heidi whispered back.

Heidi shot a quick glance at Melanie. She caught her eye by accident. Melanie stuck out her tongue. Heidi quickly looked away.

Then Mrs. Welli handed the class hat to Principal Pennypacker.

"Is everybody ready?" asked the principal.

"Yes!" shouted the class.

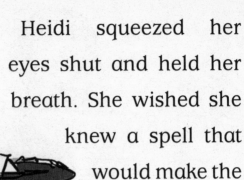

Heidi squeezed her
eyes shut and held her
breath. She wished she
knew a spell that
would make the
principal pull
out her name.

"Here we go!" said Principal
Pennypacker. He reached
into the hat and pulled
out a slip of paper.
Then he looked at
the class and said,
"Heidi Heckelbeck!"
Lucy squealed.

Melanie fell off her chair.

Heidi sat still with her eyes shut.

Lucy poked Heidi.

"Open your eyes, silly," said Lucy.

Heidi opened her eyes and let out her breath.

"Did I REALLY win the rabbit?"

"Yes, you really did!" said Lucy.

Melanie turned toward Heidi.

"That is just SO unfair," she complained. "You are way too WEIRD to take care of the rabbit."

"And you're way too mean to DESERVE the rabbit," said Lucy, who always stuck up for Heidi.

Melanie frowned and turned away.

"Congratulations, Heidi!" said Principal Pennypacker. "Please have your mom or dad pick up Maggie after school tomorrow."

Heidi nodded.

And just like that, Heidi became the keeper of the bunny.

Chapter 4

RABBiT RULES

Heidi had bunny on the brain all day Friday. She couldn't wait to take Maggie home. When Heidi's dad arrived at the school, Mrs. Welli gave Heidi a list of rules for taking care of rabbits. Heidi and Dad read them over together.

Maggie's Rabbit Rules

1. Always have plenty of fresh hay in the rabbit cage.

2. Never let the water bowl get empty.

3. At least twice a day, feed your rabbit hay, pellets, and greens. A small amount of fruit is okay on special occasions.

4. Do not feed Maggie candy, cereal, crackers, or chocolate.

5. Give Maggie an old towel to snuggle in.

6. Rabbits like to play! Make sure Maggie has her jingle ball, tunnel, and toy carrot.

7. Scoop out dirty rabbit bedding and replace it with fresh bedding as needed.

8. Never let Maggie roam around by herself. Always keep an eye on her when she's outside the cage.

"Please follow all the rules," said Mrs. Welli. "Especially the last one."

"I promise," said Heidi.

Then Heidi and her dad carried Maggie's cage to the car.

"This is going to be the best Easter ever!" Heidi said as she buckled her seat belt.

At home Mom found a cozy corner in the family room for Maggie. She laid newspaper on the floor and placed the cage on top.

"Can we take Maggie out of the cage now?" asked Heidi.

"You may only take Maggie out

of the cage when Dad or I are in the room," said Mom.

"I know," said Heidi.

"And Maggie can only be loose in a small, enclosed area," said Dad.

"I have an idea," said Heidi. "Let's use Henry's old play yard to pen Maggie in."

"Perfect," said Mom.

Dad found the play yard in the garage. He set it up in the family room. Then Heidi gently scooped Maggie from her cage and placed her inside the play yard. Mom got a bag of lettuce from the fridge and handed it to Heidi. Heidi placed a small mound of leaves in the play yard.

Hop! Hop! Hop! Maggie hopped all around. Then she nibbled on a big piece of lettuce.

"She is SO cute!" Heidi said.

"Adorable," agreed Mom.

"And SMART!" said Henry. "Like me!"

Everyone looked at Henry, who had just made a grand entrance.

He had on his magician costume, complete with white gloves and a black top hat. He pulled off his hat and held it up in the air.

"Ta-da!" said Henry. "And now I will make your bunny disappear!"

"Oh, no, you won't!" said Heidi, holding Maggie close.

"But I'll make her come back," said Henry. "I promise."

"How about you just make YOURSELF disappear?" said Heidi.

"Very funny," said Henry.

"Better yet," said Mom, "why don't you make one of your stuffed animals disappear?"

"Maybe later," Henry said. "May I hold Maggie?"

"No way," said Heidi.

"Yes way," said Mom firmly. "But you must be very gentle."

Henry sat down in the play yard. Mom spread a towel in his lap. Heidi carefully set Maggie on the towel.

"Wow," said Henry. "I can't believe we have a real, live rabbit in our house."

Heidi smiled.

"Now all we need are some Easter eggs," she said.

Chapter 5

DAZZLING DYES

On Saturday, Heidi set two cartons of hard-boiled eggs on the table in Dad's lab. Dad worked for a soda pop company called The FIZZ. He usually used his lab to invent new sodas, but today Dad created dazzling Easter egg dyes. He mixed glittery gold and

silver. He whipped up neon pink, blue, and yellow. He swirled together tie-dye colors with sparkles. Then he set out paints and brushes. He wiped his hands on his lab coat.

"We're ready!" he said.

"I'll go get everybody," said Heidi.

She ran to the living room. Mom and Henry were reading Easter stories. Aunt Trudy held Maggie in her arms.

"I see you've met Maggie," said Heidi. "Did you know she's mine for the whole weekend?"

"Wow," said Aunt Trudy. "That's one big fluffy responsibility."

"I can handle it," said Heidi.

"Of course you can," said Aunt Trudy with a wink.

Heidi smiled proudly.

"You know what?" she said. "It's time to dye Easter eggs!"

Henry jumped from the couch.

"Me first!" he shouted, and
ran toward the lab.

"Hey!" yelled Heidi. "Wait up!" She
ran after her brother. Mom and Aunt
Trudy followed behind.

Heidi and Henry each dyed six eggs. Then they painted designs on them. Heidi painted tiny bunnies on one egg and itty-bitty carrots on another. Henry drew swirls and zigzags on his eggs. Aunt Trudy dotted hers. Dad did tie-dye, and Mom speckled a whole nest full of robin's eggs.

Everyone admired one another's eggs.

"I can't wait to put my eggs in my Easter basket," said Heidi.

"And I can't wait to put mine in my lunch box," Henry said.

"Ew," said Heidi. "They'll smell like stink bombs."

"What's wrong with that?" Henry asked.

"You'll lose all your friends," said Heidi.

"No way. My friends love stink bombs," Henry said.

Everyone had things to do to get ready for Easter. Dad had to pick up the ham. Mom and Aunt Trudy had to prepare side dishes and dessert. Henry had to clean his room.

Heidi went to the family room to visit Maggie. She peeked into the cage. Maggie hopped over and stood up on her hind legs. *She wants to play,* Heidi thought. *Maybe I can take her out for a minute or two.* She knew

she wasn't supposed to take the rabbit out of the cage without a grown-up
around, but she couldn't resist. *I'll put
her right back,* she promised herself.
*Besides, everyone's so busy. They'll
never know.* Heidi checked to see if
anyone was looking. Then she slowly
unlatched the cage. . . .

Chapter 6

SiLLY WABBiT!

"Hello, little bun-bun!" Heidi said as Maggie burrowed into the crook of her arm. "I'll bet you get lonely in that crummy old cage. You want to do something fun? ME TOO!"

Then Heidi got an idea.

"Let's look at the Easter eggs!" she

said. "Come on, I'll show you."

Heidi tiptoed to the lab. She could hear Mom and Aunt Trudy chatting in the kitchen. Heidi opened the lab door with one hand. Maggie squirmed. Heidi held her more firmly.

"Voilà!" she said, showing Maggie the eggs.

Maggie squirmed some more. Heidi tried to get a better hold on the bunny, but Maggie wriggled even more. Then, *ka-boing!* She hopped right out of Heidi's arms and onto the counter. *Boing! Boing! Boing!* Maggie hopped through the bowls of egg dyes. Colors splattered everywhere! A few Easter eggs rolled onto the floor. *Crack! Crack!* Maggie hopped toward the edge of the counter.

"Oh no!" Heidi cried.

She dove to save the rabbit. Maggie landed on Heidi's back and then hopped to the floor. Heidi chased her under Dad's desk.

"Gotcha!" she said as she grabbed
Maggie around the middle.

Maggie had neon pink, blue, and yellow dyes all over her fur. Heidi had gotten splattered too. Puddles of dyes covered the counter and dripped onto the floor.

"What have I done?" she cried. "I'm in BIG trouble. I need to clean up this mess FAST!"

She set Maggie in a deep sink to keep her safe. Then she sponged the dyes off the counter and the floor. She picked up the eggs. They had spider cracks everywhere.

"Oh, Maggie!" cried Heidi. "How COULD you?"

She put the eggs in the wastebasket and covered them with paper towels. Then she lifted the

tie-dyed Maggie from the sink.

"We'd better get out of here before we get caught," said Heidi.

She slipped out the door and looked both ways. Then she raced upstairs

to her bedroom and zoomed into the
bathroom. Heidi grabbed a bottle of
baby shampoo and put Maggie in the
sink.

"Time for a bunny bath," she said.

SCRUB-A-
DUB-DUB

Heidi squeezed shampoo onto
Maggie's fur and then lathered it
with a cup of warm water. Then she
checked Maggie's fur. The dyes were
still there. Heidi poured on more
shampoo, but Maggie scrambled
out of the sink and onto the counter.

She scampered across the tiles and knocked over the soap dish. Heidi grabbed her and put her back in the sink.

"Sit still!" Heidi said. "Don't you know we're in HUGE trouble?"

Heidi scrubbed some more. But it was no use. The dyes would not come out.

Heidi then rinsed the soap from Maggie's fur. Maggie shivered.

"Hang on, fur ball," Heidi said. "It's time for our backup plan."

Heidi wrapped Maggie in a towel and hurried to her bedroom. She knew she wasn't supposed to practice her spells without asking, but this was an emergency. Heidi pulled her *Book of Spells* from under the bed. She flipped through the pages until she found a chapter called "Stain Removal from *A* to *Z*."

"Oh, thank goodness!" Heidi said.

She read through the list of stains:
*barbecue sauce, blood, chocolate,
coffee, dessert, dirt . . . DYE!* She flipped
to the spell and looked it over.

How to Cast Out Dye

Do your colors bleed in the washing machine? Have you ever dyed your hair purple and then changed your mind? Has Easter egg dye ever wound up on something besides the eggs? Don't cry over spilled dye! This is the spell for you!

Ingredients:
1 pea-size squirt of white toothpaste
1 teaspoon of sugar
1 cup of ginger ale

Combine the ingredients in a large cup. Blend with a wire whisk. Apply potion to stain. Hold your Witches of Westwick medallion in your left hand. Hold your right hand over the stain. Chant the following words:

FIDDLE DEE DOO!
FIDDLE DEE DEE!
LET THIS [NAME OF OBJECT]
BE STAIN FREE!

Perfect, thought Heidi. *All I have to do is gather the ingredients. But first I have to make sure Maggie's safe.* Heidi emptied her toy crate. Then she lined the bottom with her old baby blanket. She fluffed Maggie's wet fur with the towel and gently lowered her into the crate.

Heidi changed into a clean shirt and skirt. Then she bolted downstairs.

Chapter 8

GOiNG DOTTY

Heidi took a peek into the kitchen. *Uh-oh*, she thought. *Everyone's in there.* Aunt Trudy had the mixer on. Henry and Mom were sitting at the table and snapping beans. Dad was slicing the ham.

Okay, thought Heidi. *Just act*

natural. She strolled into the kitchen and walked to the cupboard. Then she pulled out a measuring cup.

"Hi, sweetie," Mom said. "Would you like to join us?"

"No, thanks," said Heidi as she pulled a bottle of ginger ale from the fridge. "Just getting a drink."

"In a measuring cup?" asked Aunt Trudy.

Heidi poured ginger ale up to the one-cup line. "Don't want to drink too much soda," she said.

Then Heidi
poured the
ginger ale from
the measuring
cup into a
tall glass.

Mom and
Aunt Trudy
exchanged glances.

Heidi sat at the table
and added a teaspoon of sugar to her
ginger ale.

"Mom, Heidi just put sugar in her
ginger ale!" said Henry.

Mom frowned.

"What's the big deal?" Heidi said innocently. "It's sugar free. It needs a little sugar."

"You're weird," said Henry.

Heidi shrugged and grabbed a whisk from the utensil holder. Then she scooted out of the kitchen.

"That girl is up to some-thing," she heard Aunt Trudy say.

"She sure is," said Mom.

Heidi raced upstairs with her glass. *I'd*

better hurry before I get caught, she thought. She ran to the bathroom and squeezed a pea-size glob of toothpaste into the cup. The toothpaste had little blue specks in it. Then she whisked the potion. She grabbed her Witches of Westwick medallion and

sat next to her toy crate. Heidi carefully drizzled the potion on Maggie
and spread it over the stains. Then
Heidi held her medallion in her left
hand and placed her right hand on
top of Maggie. She chanted the spell.

FiDDLE DEE DOO!
FiDDLE DEE DEE!
LET THiS RABBiT
BE STAiN FREE!

Heidi lifted her hand from the bunny and looked down. Her eyes got wide. Then she cupped her hand over her mouth.

"Oh no!" Heidi cried. "What have I done?"

Maggie was white with blue polka dots.

"I can't take you back to school looking like THIS!"

Heidi picked up Maggie and wrapped her in the old baby blanket.

There was only one thing left to do.

Get help.

Chapter 9

RABBiT EARS

Heidi carried Maggie downstairs. *Boy, am I going to get it,* she thought. But she had no choice. She had to tell Mom and Aunt Trudy. They were the two best witches she knew. Heidi stood in the doorway of the family room. Mom and Aunt Trudy were relaxing and drinking tea. They looked up when they saw Heidi.

"Heidi, what's Maggie doing out of her cage?" Mom asked.

Heidi bit her lip. "Mom, I did something really bad," she said.

Mom and Aunt Trudy looked at each other.

"Does it have to do with Maggie being out of the cage?" asked Mom.

Maggie squirmed in the towel.

"Yes," said Heidi.

"Okay, out with it," said Mom.

Heidi took a deep breath. "I wanted to show Maggie the Easter eggs."

"And?" Mom asked.

"And then she jumped out of my arms and spilled the Easter egg dyes," Heidi explained. "The dyes stained her fur, and I couldn't get them out."

Mom sighed.

"It gets worse," said Heidi.

She unwrapped the blanket.

"I used a stain removal spell, and look what happened."

Mom gasped.

Aunt Trudy tried not to laugh. "What kind of toothpaste did you use in the spell?" she asked.

"The white-with-blue-speckles kind," said Heidi.

"Well, that explains the blue polka dots," Aunt Trudy said.

"Can we fix it?" asked Heidi.

"That depends," said Mom.

"On what?" Heidi asked.

"If you can promise to follow the Rabbit Rules for the rest of the weekend."

"I cross my heart and hope to obey

ALL rules for the rest of my life," said Heidi.

"Then perhaps we can find a solution," said Mom.

"It's not that simple," said Aunt Trudy, who practiced her witching skills more often than Heidi's mom. "There's one ingredient that may be hard to find."

"What?" asked Heidi.

"The ears of a

white-chocolate rabbit," said Aunt Trudy.

"Do they even make rabbits out of white-chocolate?" Heidi asked.

"Yes," said Aunt Trudy. "But not as many as milk-chocolate and dark-chocolate rabbits."

"And Easter is tomorrow," added Mom. "They might be sold out."

"I'll take a look this evening," said Aunt Trudy. "If I can find a white rabbit, we can change Maggie back tomorrow."

"Oh, thank you, Aunt Trudy," said
Heidi. "I'm sorry I caused so much
trouble."

"That's why we have rules," said Mom.

Heidi nodded.

Aunt Trudy put on her coat and patted Maggie on the way out.

"Maybe you should call her Dot," she said with a wink.

"Not funny," said Heidi.

Henry walked in from the kitchen. "What's not funny?" he asked while nibbling on some ham.

"Don't ask," said Heidi.

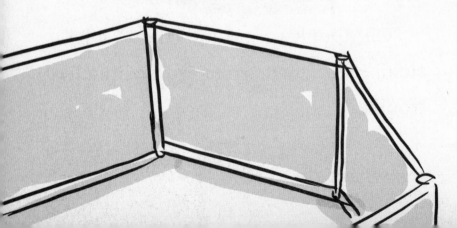

Chapter 10

HOPPY EASTER!

"Ready? On your mark! Get set! GO!" shouted Dad.

Heidi and Henry clutched their Easter baskets and raced into the backyard. Henry grabbed plastic eggs from the birdbath, from the flower-pots, and from all along the fence.

Heidi tried to keep up, but her mind was on Maggie. Aunt Trudy hadn't called yet to say she'd found a white-chocolate rabbit for the spell. *What if she doesn't find one?* thought Heidi. *I can't go back to Brewster Elementary with a polka-dot rabbit!*

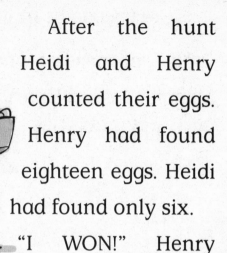

After the hunt Heidi and Henry counted their eggs. Henry had found eighteen eggs. Heidi had found only six.

"I WON!" Henry shouted. "For the first time in history, I beat you!"

Heidi shrugged. "I let you win," she said.

"You would NEVER just LET me win," said Henry.

"True," said Heidi. "But I did today."

"Is it because of what happened to Maggie?" asked Henry.

"What do YOU think?" said Heidi.

"I think this year's first prize goes to Henry!" interrupted Dad as he handed him a giant chocolate chicken.

Heidi got a small chocolate chicken.

"I'm glad I didn't get a chocolate RABBIT," said Heidi gloomily. "I'd rather not think about rabbits, let alone eat one."

Heidi didn't play with Maggie all morning. She couldn't bear to look at her polka-dot fur. It only reminded her of the mess she was in.

At noon the doorbell rang.

"I'll get it!" Heidi shouted. She opened the door to find Aunt Trudy. She was smiling and carrying a brown grocery bag in her arms.

"I had to go to five stores," she said.

"Did you find one?" asked Heidi.

Aunt Trudy pulled a white-chocolate rabbit out of the bag.

"It was the only one that was

completely white," she said.

Heidi hugged her aunt. "You are the BEST!" she said. "Can we change Maggie back?"

"The sooner the better," said Aunt Trudy. "Get your *Book of Spells* and medallion."

Heidi ran to her room and grabbed her *Book of Spells* and Witches of Westwick medallion.

Aunt Trudy opened the book to Chapter Ten: "Cuddly Critters." Heidi and Mom gathered the ingredients for the spell. Then Aunt Trudy melted the white-chocolate rabbit's ears in a saucepan. She added a half cup of lemon juice, a quarter teaspoon of salt, and a

tablespoon of sage. Then she placed polka-dot Maggie in the sink. When the mixture had cooled, she spread the  potion over Maggie's fur. She held Heidi's medallion in her left hand and gently placed her right hand over Maggie. Heidi and Mom watched as Aunt Trudy chanted the spell.

SNOWFLAKES, CLOUDS,
AND WINTER LIGHT—
MAKE MAGGIE'S FUR
PEARLY AND WHITE.

Aunt Trudy lifted her hand. Maggie
looked as white as a cotton ball.

"You did it!" Heidi cried.

"You mean I *un*did it," Aunt Trudy
said.

Heidi hugged her aunt. "I'm so
sorry this happened," she said.

"Did you learn something?" Mom asked.

"I sure did," said Heidi. "I learned that I really REALLY want my very own pet."

Aunt Trudy and Mom frowned.

"How about we recover from this pet experience first?" Mom said.

Heidi hung her head.

"And we'll think about it," said Mom.

Heidi called Dad and Henry in for their Easter meal. Then she gave Maggie a slice of apple as a special treat.

"I don't want to take you back to school tomorrow," Heidi said. "But at least you're the right color."

Chapter 11

SPOTLESS!

Mom and Heidi carried Maggie's cage to Principal Pennypacker's office. Mom gave Heidi a hug good-bye and went on her way.

"How did it go, Heidi?" asked the principal as he opened the cage and lifted Maggie into his arms.

"Great," said Heidi.

The principal pet Maggie's fur.

"Her coat looks very shiny and clean," he said. "Did you give her a bath?"

"Just a little one," said Heidi, trying not to make too much of it.

Then Principal Pennypacker stopped petting Maggie and raised an eyebrow.

"What's wrong?" asked Heidi.

"Well, I could've sworn Maggie had a brown spot behind her left ear," said the principal.

Heidi gulped. "Uh, I never noticed a brown spot," she said.

"That's odd," he said. "I must've imagined it."

Then he nuzzled Maggie against his cheek. "Oh my," he said. "Do I smell sage?"

Heidi laughed nervously. "Um, I'd better go to class," she said. "I don't want to be late."

Principal Pennypacker looked curiously at Heidi.

"Yes," he said. "You'd better run along."

Heidi hurried to the door. On the way out, she noticed a large black book sticking out of Principal Pennypacker's bag.

It had gold writing on the spine. *Wow, that actually looks a lot like my* Book of Spells, she thought.

Then a funny feeling came over Heidi as she walked down the hall. *Does Principal Pennypacker know what happened to Maggie?* she wondered.

The thought made her shiver. *But how could he? Unless . . . Could it be?*

Heidi swallowed.

Could Principal Pennypacker be . . . a WITCH?

Check out the next book starring

HEIDI HECKELBECK

At school Heidi told Lucy Lancaster about the the flower girl dress.

"You're so lucky!" Lucy exclaimed. "I've always wanted to be in a wedding."

"Want to trade places?" asked Heidi.

"Very funny," said Lucy. "So, what does your dress look like?"

"I brought a picture," Heidi said.

An excerpt from *Heidi Heckelbeck Is a Flower Girl*

"But promise not to laugh."

"Promise," said Lucy.

Heidi reached into her back pocket and pulled out the picture. She started to hand it to Lucy, but Melanie snatched it out of Heidi's hand.

"Let ME see!" cried Melanie.

"Hey, that's MINE!" cried Heidi.

Melanie looked at the picture and squealed with laughter.

"Oh my gosh, that dress is SO icky!" cried Melanie in between laughs.

Stanley Stonewrecker snuck up behind Melanie and grabbed the picture out of her hand.

"Wow, Heidi," said Stanley as he handed the picture to Lucy. "You look great in that dress."

Melanie folded her arms and turned up her nose. "I'll bet Heidi won't even be able to walk in that dress," said Melanie. "She'll probably trip and fall when she walks down the aisle."

Heidi couldn't believe what Melanie had just said. It was as if she knew Heidi had had a bad dream about falling down at the wedding. *How does she do that?* Heidi thought. *And what if I really do fall down in front of everybody?*

An excerpt from *Heidi Heckelbeck Is a Flower Girl*